Written by Gaby Goldsack
Illustrated by Frank Endersby
Language consultant: Betty Root

This is a Parragon Book
First published in 2002

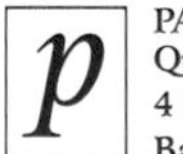
PARRAGON
Queen Street House
4 Queen Street
Bath BA1 1HE

ISBN 0-75258-179-1

Printed in China

Farmer Fred

and the Greedy Crows

p

It was milking time on Bluebell Farm and Farmer Fred was on his way to the cowshed. Betty, Farmer Fred's wife, came out of the farmhouse. She was wearing her smart clothes to go to town.

"I'm off to Sunnybridge to do some shopping, Fred," she called to him. "Is there anything you need from town?"

"No thanks," said Farmer Fred. "You look very smart, dear!"

"Thank you," said Betty. "You look like a scarecrow!"

"But I always dress like this," said Farmer Fred looking down at his patched dungarees.

"That must be why you always look like a scarecrow," laughed Betty.

Later, Farmer Fred was in the milking parlour singing along to the radio when Patch the sheepdog raced in.

"Woof!" barked Patch.

"What is it?" asked Farmer Fred, looking puzzled.

Patch barked again, then Farmer Fred followed him out of the barn.

He followed Patch across the yard. He could hear loud squawks coming from the cornfield. He began to run.

"Not those...

...greedy crows again!" he cried. And, sure enough, a flock of crows was pecking away at Farmer Fred's lovely corn.

"Get away, you greedy crows!" shouted Farmer Fred, waving his arms about.

"Woof!" barked Patch.

"Caw!" squawked the crows. They weren't going to let Farmer Fred and Patch spoil their feast!

Farmer Fred raced around the field flapping his arms about. Patch chased first one crow, then another. But the crows just flew out of the way and went back to their corn feast.

"Can't catch us!" cawed the greedy crows.

Farmer Fred and Patch ran round and round in circles, until they felt quite dizzy and had to sit down.

"Stop eating all my corn!" shouted Farmer Fred as he waved a fist at the crows.

"Cooee!" squawked the crows, laughing at Farmer Fred.

"I've got an idea!" said Farmer Fred suddenly. "I know just what will get rid of those greedy crows!" And he ran off across the field and disappeared into his workshop.

Soon, the air was filled with the sounds of hammering and sawing. All the farm animals came to see what was happening.

"Uh-oh!" said Penny the pig. "It sounds like Farmer Fred is making something. And that usually means trouble."

"Well, he's certainly making something," said Charlie the cockerel, who was looking in through the workshop window. "But I don't know what it is. I've never seen anything like it!"

Tap! Tap! Tap!
Sssss! Sssss!

Hours later, the workshop door swung open and a strange-looking machine rattled into sight.

"Introducing the Thingymajig!" cried Farmer Fred from behind the steering wheel. He looked very pleased with himself.

The animals ran for cover as the Thingymajig crashed, banged and walloped its way across the yard towards the cornfield.

"Look out, you greedy crows!" chuckled Farmer Fred. "Here I come!"

"This will put a stop to your nonsense!" Farmer Fred shouted to the crows. He pulled a heavy lever and turned a huge dial. Out shot two tennis balls and an arrow.

"Woof!" Patch warned, as the tennis ball bounced once on Penny's bottom and landed in the the water barrel. Another ball nearly hit the crows but they just ducked. An arrow whizzed through the air, then stuck to Chloe the cow's nose. Penny and Chloe were very cross.

"This isn't going to work!" thought Patch.

"Caw!" laughed the crows. "What is Farmer Fred playing at?"

...collapsed into a heap!

"Caw! Caw! Caw!" laughed the crows. "That was very funny, Farmer Fred!"

Patch helped Farmer Fred out of the duck pond. Farmer Fred was *soaked* from head to toe.

"It looks like I'll never get rid of those greedy crows," *said* Farmer Fred.

Farmer Fred trudged back to the farm house. He emptied out his wellington boots, then took off his hat and dungarees. He was just hanging them on an old rake handle to dry, when Betty arrived home from market.

"Oh dear!" said Betty, seeing Farmer Fred standing at the farmhouse door, dripping. "Whatever happened to you?"

"It's a long story," sighed Farmer Fred. "But the short of it is that I fell in the duck pond!"

"It's a good thing I bought you these, then," smiled Betty. And she gave Farmer Fred a bag.

Farmer Fred pulled open the bag. Betty had bought him a new hat, shirt, dungarees and wellington boots.

"Woof!" barked Patch as he picked up an old boot. Farmer Fred looked at his new clothes, and looked at his old clothes. Then he remembered what Betty had said that morning.

Farmer Fred grabbed both sets of clothes and charged across the yard.

"I've got an idea!" he shouted. And for the second time that day, he disappeared into his workshop.

Five minutes later, the workshop door swung open and Farmer Fred came out carrying...

...a scarecrow wearing his old clothes. Patch and Farmer Fred carried it down to the cornfield.

The crows took one look at the scarecrow and disappeared in fright.

"I knew I'd think of something," said Farmer Fred.

"Woof!" barked Patch, wagging his tail as the crows flew away. Betty smiled.